THE LOST CHRISTMAS LETTERS

Written and Illustrated by

Debbie Dearen Richmond

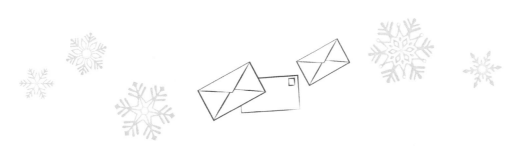

Published by Words to Ponder Publishing, LLC

Illustrations and story created by Debbie Dearen Richmond

Manuscript written by Debbie Dearen Richmond

Book design by Sofania Delarte

First Print

Library of Congress Control Number: 2020908243

Address of inquiries to Contact@florenza.org

eBook ISBN 978-1-941328-33-0

Softcover ISBN 978-1-941328-34-7

Hardcover ISBN 978-1-941328-35-4

Words to Ponder Publishing Company, LLC

Printed in the United States of America

For more information, visit https://www.florenza.org.

This Book Belongs To:

_____

*I dedicate this book to Will, Charlie,
Cate, Caroline, and Wright.
May you always believe in the spirit
of Christmas.*

Deeds

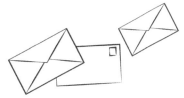

"Only two more weeks until Christmas!" announced the cubs as they diligently worked on their Christmas lists.

"This year, I want a toy train AND a football!" said Charles, while tucking his list into an envelope.

"I… I'm almost done," said Merry, whose list wrapped around her sheet of paper. "I just need to add one more thing: To Santa With Love! There, done!"

Preston paced the room.

"You cubs better get going to the mailbox, before the snow starts!" Mother said, as she glanced out the cave opening.

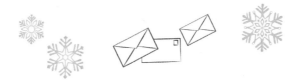

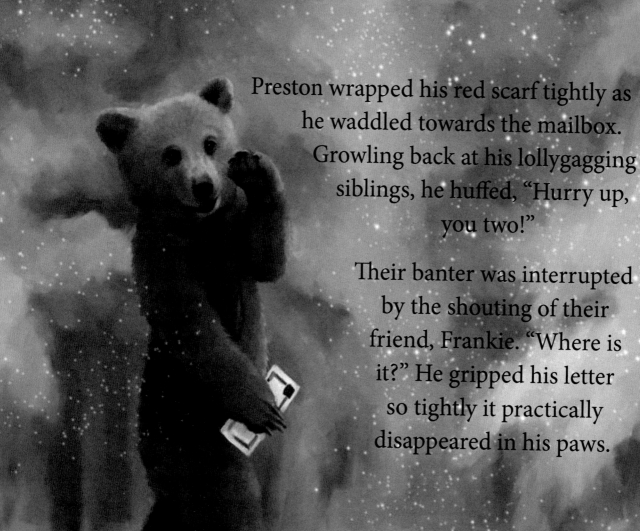

Preston wrapped his red scarf tightly as he waddled towards the mailbox. Growling back at his lollygagging siblings, he huffed, "Hurry up, you two!"

Their banter was interrupted by the shouting of their friend, Frankie. "Where is it?" He gripped his letter so tightly it practically disappeared in his paws.

"The mailbox is gone?" Preston shook his head back and forth. "Last night's storm must have blown it away!"

"Oh, that's just great! Now Santa won't get our letters in time for Christmas!" Merry huffed.

"Or these," said Charles as he hurried to pick up scattered envelopes. They were addressed to the North Pole. "Maybe… WE should take them to him!"

Franky chuckled as he gathered the last envelope. "Take them to who? Santa? We don't know where he lives."

"Well, WE don't, but I bet Mr. Beaver the mailman might!" said Merry.

A mighty whinny carried through the forest as Cody galloped towards them.

"Santa's missing letters! I have searched far and wide; I knew that I would find them! Santa has been so dismayed; he thought the children forgot to write their letters."

Together they loaded all the letters into the sacks,
and hoisted them onto Cody's back. The group
headed off into the forest. And then…
snow began to fall even *harder*.

Cody?" Merry called through the snowflakes.
"Do you know where you are going?"

"I... well, I was following my own tracks back,
but it seems now they are covered!"

"Hello," a friendly voice called as antlers emerged through the snow.

"Dillon! We are glad to see you!" Charles gave him a big bear hug.

"We are on our way to deliver lost letters to Santa!"

"Well, I can't tell you how to find Santa, but I can help by carrying some of those."

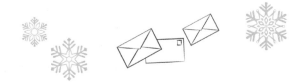

As they journeyed further, a painful howl
cried out from the trees.

"Wendy?" Merry questioned as she neared her den.

"I went to the mailbox to drop off the letters from my
pack, and it was gone! Now, none of the wolves will get
their letters to the North Pole in time," she sobbed.

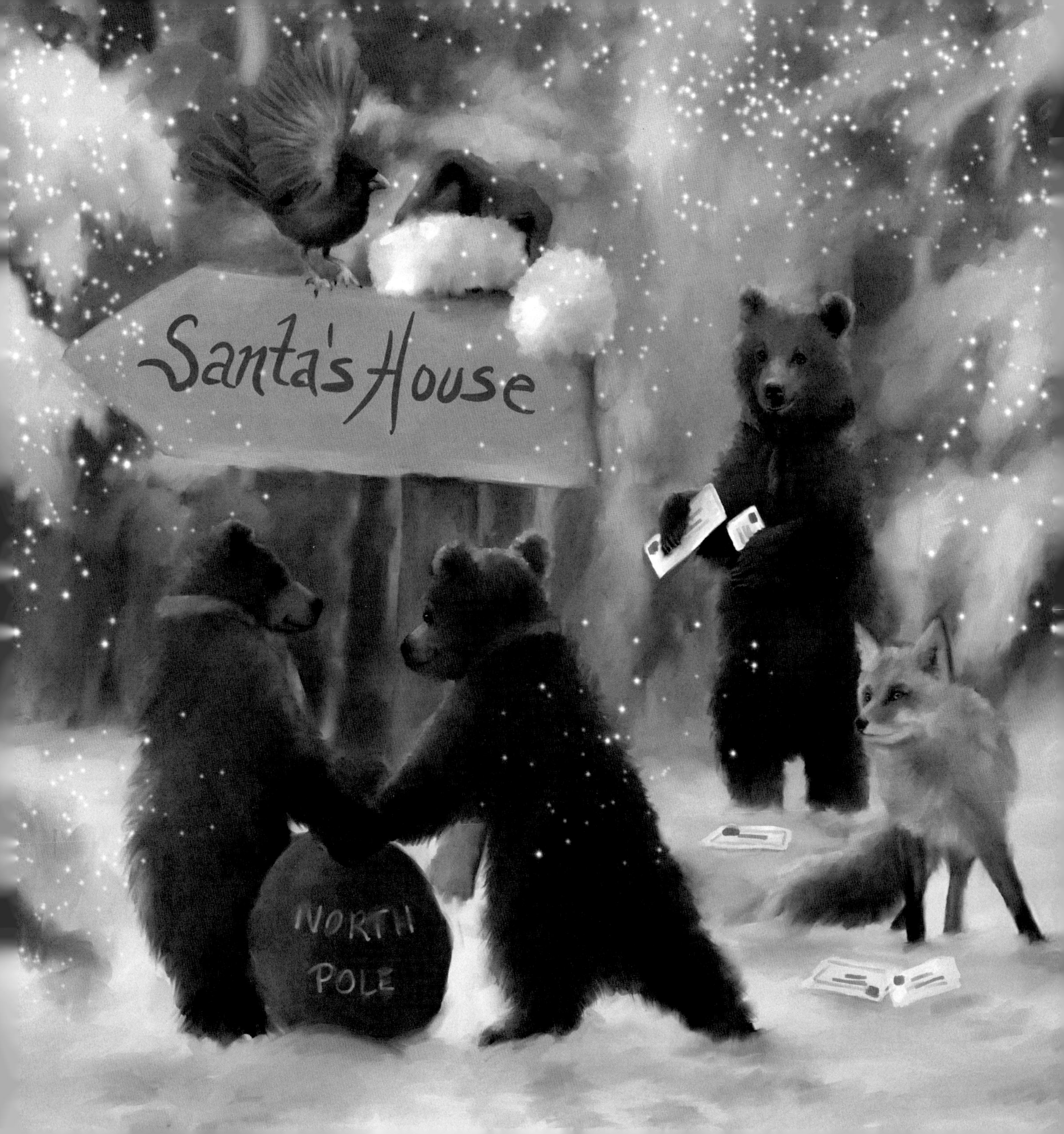
Santa's House
NORTH POLE

Just then, something red zipped through the snow,
singing cheerful news.

"Follow me, don't delay! I know the way to Santa's place."

All eyes lifted upward as Mr. Cardinal flew off in the distance,
towards a smokestack pouring
out from a chimney.

Over the hills, on the brink of the piney forest, a log house stood. Together the three cubs knocked on the door and took a step back as the wooden door creaked open.

Santa cheerfully bellowed a welcoming "Ho! Ho! Ho!"

Wide-eyed, they shouted, "SANTA!"

"Hello, Preston, Merry, Charles, Franky, Dillon, Wendy, and Cody."

"The storm blew away the mailboxes," said Merry, but we knew we couldn't let that keep you from getting these letters.

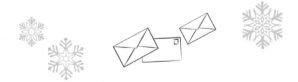

"This is the true Christmas spirit, indeed, going out of your way to bring joy to others. You must be exhausted from your journey. May I offer you something to eat?"

They nodded happily and gathered around the fire.

Santa reached into his bag of goodies.

"These are no ordinary apples; they come from Mrs. Claus' garden! She claims they keep you full of gratitude all year long."

"But… there's one extra." Preston attempted to return it to Santa.

"That one is for Mother Bear, she's been worried about all of you."

After they returned home, they excitedly told Mother Bear of the
lost letters, an unexpected journey, and how
Santa said they saved Christmas.
As she tucked them safely into bed,
Preston said, "This is a
special apple for you."

The cubs snuggled closely. Preston asked, "Can you believe we actually got to meet Santa at his farm?"

"That was awesome," giggled Merry.

"Do you know what my favorite part of today was?" smiled Berry. "Knowing that our journey helped all of the forest animals to have a very Merry Christmas."

THE END

DEBBIE DEAREN RICHMOND

ABOUT THE AUTHOR

Debbie Richmond lives in Memphis, TN, and has been an artist for over 30 years. She and her husband own the Blue Plate Cafes and Gallery. She has two daughters and five grandchildren, two Labs, and two Great Dane puppies. Debbie has been an avid golfer for more than four decades.

Decorating and celebrating Christmas is one of Debbie's favorite seasons. "The Big Christmas Adventure" is her first venture as a children's picture book author, and illustrator. Therefore, it is not surprising that her first book would combine the two.

Debbie has won numerous art awards over her career, and specializes in wildlife and animal portraits at her Pointe South Studio. She's a Signature Member of Women Artists of the West, Oil Painters of America, and Society of Children's Book Writers and Illustrators.

"I genuinely enjoy painting still life and landscapes, but painting animals is my passion. The greatest joy an artist can receive is to capture the personality, a moment in time, and the facial expressions that only one who loves animals can understand in a portrait. I find the eyes are the heart and soul into telling an animal's story. When a viewer says they felt a connection through a dog's loving gaze, a deer's startled glance, or the penetration of a tiger's glare, I know I've accomplished my mission."

We thank you for inviting us into your homes, schools, libraries, cars, park benches, your beach chair, and more.

If you have enjoyed reading our books, kindly leave us a review on Amazon.com or GoodReads.com.

We would love to hear from you; as a reminder, we are available for in-person and virtual events. You may follow us on any of our social media sites. You may also email us at the follow addresses:

Florenza – Contact@florenza.org

Debbie - ddrichmondart@aol.com

We have more books to share, and hope you will continue to support us at Words to Ponder Publishing, LLC.

Happy reading!

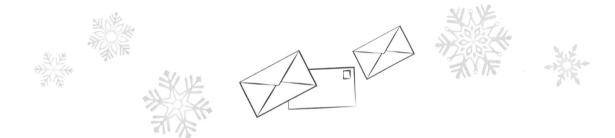

Made in the USA
Columbia, SC
02 November 2021

48237155R00027